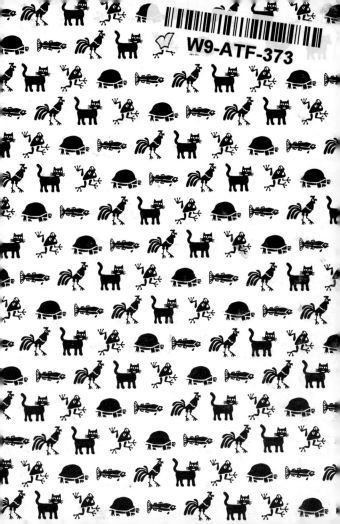

SIMON & SCHUSTER BOOKS FOR YOUNG READERS
An imprint of Simon & Schuster Children's Publishing Division
1230 Avenue of the Americas
New York, New York 10020
Copyright © 1972 by Eric Carle

Simon & Schuster Books for Young Readers is a trademark of Simon & Schus
Printed in Indonesia
4 6 8 10 9 7 5

Library of Congress Cataloging in Publication Data
Carle, Eric.
[Rooster who set out to see the world]
Rooster's off to see the world/by Eric Carle.
p. cm. — (Pixies)
Summary: A simple introduction to the meaning of numbers and sets as a roo
on his way to see the world, is joined by fourteen animals along the way.
ISBN 0-88708-178-9 : $4.95
[1. Numbers. 2. Counting. 3. Animals—Fiction] I. Title. II. Series.
PZ7.C21476Ro 1991
[E]—dc20 91-15246
CIP
AC

Rooster's Off
to See the World

ERIC CARLE

Simon & Schuster Books for Young Readers

One fine morning,
a rooster decided that he wanted to travel.
So, right then and there, he set out to see the world.
He hadn't walked very far when he began to feel lone

st then, he met two cats. The rooster said to
em, "Come along with me to see the world."
e cats liked the idea of a trip very much.
e would love to," they purred and set
f down the road with the rooster.

s they wandered on, the rooster and the cats
et three frogs. "How would you like to
ome with us to see the world?" asked
e rooster, eager for more company.
'hy not?" answered the frogs.
'e are not busy now." So the
ogs jumped along behind the
ooster and the cats.

After a while, the rooster, the cats, and the frogs
saw four turtles crawling slowly down the road.
"Hey," said the rooster, "how would you
like to see the world?"
"It might be fun," snapped one of
the turtles and they joined
the others.

s the rooster, the cats, the frogs, and the
urtles walked along, they came to five fish
swimming in the brook.
"Where are you going?" asked the fish.
"We're off to see the world,"
answered the rooster.
"May we come along?"
pleaded the fish.
"Delighted to have you,"
the rooster replied.

And so the fish came along to see the world.

The sun went down. It began to get dark. The moon came up over the horizon. "Where's our dinner?" asked the cats. "Where are we supposed to sleep?" asked the frogs. "We're cold," complained the turtles

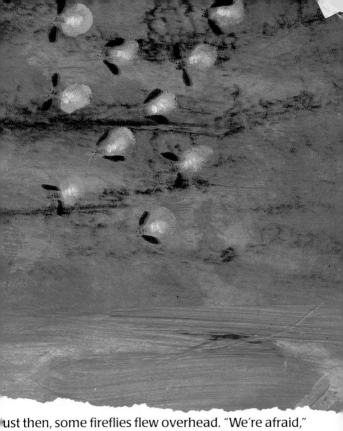

ust then, some fireflies flew overhead. "We're afraid," cried the fish. Now, the rooster really had not made any plans for the trip around the world. He had not remembered to think about food and shelter, so he didn't know how to answer his friends.

After a few minutes of silen
the fish suddenly decide
that it might be best if they heade
for home. They wished the othe
a happy trip and swam awa

Then, the turtles began to think
about their warm house
They turned and crawled back
down the road without
so much as a good-bye

The frogs weren't too happy with the tri
anymore, either. First one and the
the other and finally the last on
jumped away. They were polit
enough, though, to wis
the rooster a good evenin
as they disappeared into the nigh

The cats then remembered an unfinished meal
they had left behind. They kindly wished
the rooster a happy journey
and they, too, headed for home.
Now the rooster was all alone
and he hadn't seen anything
of the world. He thought for a minute
and then said to the moon:
"To tell you the truth, I am not only hungry
and cold, but I'm homesick as well."
The moon did not answer.
It, too, disappeared.

The rooster knew what he had to do. He turned aroun
and went back home again. He enjoyed a good mea
of grain and then sat on his very own perch.

After a while he went to sleep and had a wonderful
happy dream—all about a trip around the world!

As a child, Eric Carle claims to have been much more of a philosopher than a mathematician. He recalls his difficulties this way:

"If you told me that there were two apples in a bowl and one was taken away and then asked me how many apples were left I wasn't sure. After all, you can't really take away an apple. You can eat it or make cider out of it or hide it under a basket, but the apple is still an apple and it isn't really gone...

"On the other hand, if you added one apple to a bowl with an apple already in it, there was always the bowl to worry about. Wasn't that a something to count in the total?"

Eric Carle wrote Rooster's Off to See the World not only for the child who has these difficulties with numbers and specific symbols, but also for all children who are getting acquainted with numbers.